Elbert Hubbard, Adeline Knapp

Upland Pastures

Elbert Hubbard, Adeline Knapp

Upland Pastures

ISBN/EAN: 9783337366698

Printed in Europe, USA, Canada, Australia, Japan

Cover: Foto ©Andreas Hilbeck / pixelio.de

More available books at **www.hansebooks.com**

THIS THEN IS

UPLAND PASTURES

BEING SOME OUT-DOOR ESSAYS DEALING WITH THE BEAUTIFUL THINGS THAT THE SPRING AND SUMMER BRING ☘ ☘ ☘

By ADELINE KNAPP

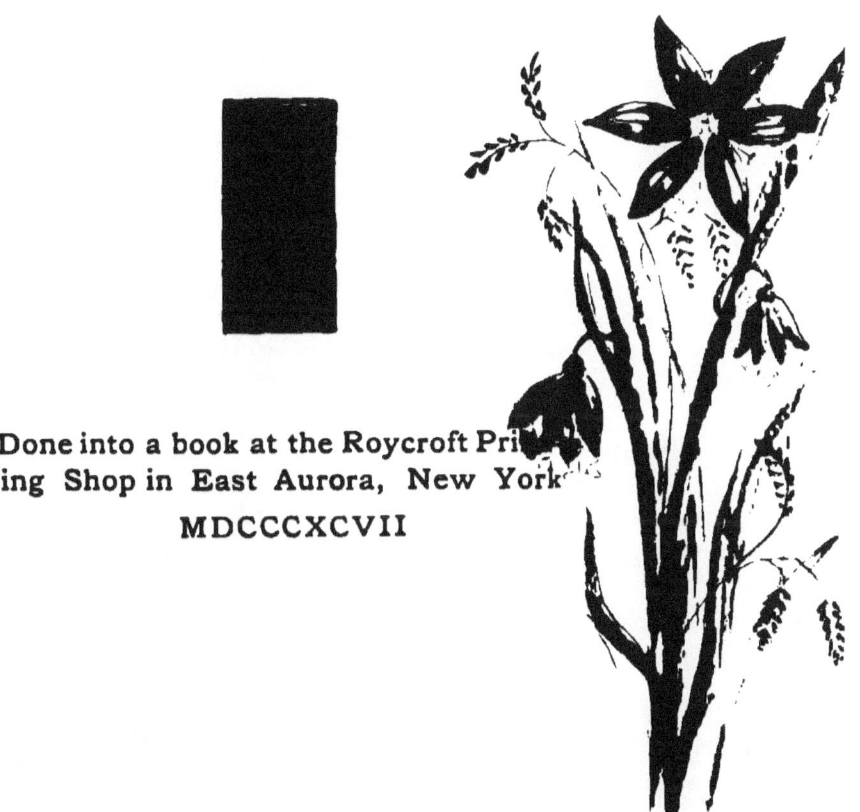

Done into a book at the Roycroft Printing Shop in East Aurora, New York
MDCCCXCVII

OF THIS EDITION THERE WERE PRINTED BUT SIX HUNDRED COPIES ☘ EACH BOOK IS SIGNED AND NUMBERED: THIS BOOK IS NUMBER

HEN the warm rains succeed winter's driving downpours, and the young grass begins to mantle the meadows with tender green, is the time, of all the year, to be out of doors. All the woodsy places are cool and dripping and dim and delicious. A month later they will be not less beautiful, perhaps, but less approachable. The things of Nature grow sophisticated as the season advances. In the early springtime they are frank and confiding, and willingly tell the secrets of their growth to him who asks. They have time, in these first beginnings of things, for friendly sociability: to show their tiny roots and bulbs, and let us study the delicate, gracious unfoldings of leaf and bud and blossom. In a few weeks they will all be too busy, keeping up with the season's swift march, to stop and visit with the lovingest of human friends. Do we forget, from springtime to springtime, how lovely will be the year's awakening? Each winter of our discontent I think to remember, as my longing imagination looks forward, the tender charm of the springtime wonder, yet with each recurring year it comes to me as a new and unknown joy.

The whole world seems to welcome the new year-child. Even before the first growths appear there is a hushed awareness throughout Nature that moves the heart to thankfulness and remembered expectation ❦ The hope of springtime comes without stint, and without fail, bringing each one of us the message his heart is prepared to receive, and quickening our purest, least sordid impulses. The best that is in us seems possible, in the springtime. Who of us does not then dream that this best will yet gain strength to withstand the heat and drouth of summer's fierce searching? We turn to Mother Nature like children who long to be good. The worshipping instinct that lies deep within each soul goes out to her, vesting her in that personality which we have long since pronounced unthinkable when applied to God. There is a suggestion in the situation that is not without a certain saving humor to relieve it from grotesqueness. We are not far from a personal god when we send our souls out in loving contemplation of personified Nature, yet we still go on asking if God is, and if He is Truth. Whom do we ask, and why does the question rise? If God is Truth, He must be universal; and to be perceived by each soul for himself ❦ If, then, I perceive him not, either He is not the truth or else I am simple and sincere in desiring the truth. If He is not the truth, do I then desire human persuasion that He is? Or, if I am not simple and sincere, who can make me so?

NATURE will help us if we turn to her. We have filled our lives so full of complexities and problems that it is well for us to have her annual reminder that even without our taking thought about it the real world, that will be here when we, with all our busyness, shall have passed from sight, has renewed itself, and stands bidding us come and find peace. For Nature keeps open house for us, and even when we visit her and leave a trail of dust and desolation behind us, like the stupid, untidy children we are, she only sets herself, with the silent, persistent patience of her age-wise motherhood, to cover and remove it. Down in the canyon, this morning, among the trillium and loosestrife and wild potato, I found the inevitable tin can left by some picnicker to mar and desecrate the landscape, but now completely filled with soft brown mold, and growing in it a mass of happy green wood-sorrel

This is better than going at things with a broom, gathering them up and removing them from one place to another, which is about as far as we humans have progressed in our science of cleaning up I was glad to welcome the trillium. How one loves its quaint old name of wake-robin, fitting title for this first harbinger of spring, that comes to us even before the robin's note is heard. Many of our common wild-flowers have several names, but there is none with such invariably pretty ones as all ages have united in bestowing upon wake-robin. Birth-root, our forefathers called it, seeing the birth of the new year in its early blossoming, and how many generations have known it as the trinity-flower! But 'tis best known, I think, as wake-robin, and the very breath of spring is in the name.

A MEMBER of the great lily family is wake-robin. It loves damp, shady places and moist, rich valleys. On the Pacific Coast we do not find the typical Eastern variety, but we have a variety of our own, tho' unmistakably wake-robin. Its color varies from rich madder-red to pale-pink, sometimes almost white. It grows from a thick, tuber-like root, and the calyx has, surrounding its three red petals and three green sepals, three broad, mottled-green leaves which, for some unaccountable reason, our florists remove when they offer the flower for sale. A strange whimsy, this. The poor blossoms, thus denuded, have a bewildered, self-conscious air, such as may have been worn by the little egg-selling woman of old, who awoke from her nap by the king's highway to find her petticoats shorn. Well may wake-robin thus question its own identity. It is no longer the trillium of the forest: it is only the trillium of commerce, a sad, unlovely object.

A bank where wake-robin lifts its bonny head is always fair to see. The plant has certain boon companions always sure to be close at hand. The Solomon's seal is one of these, its roots bearing to this day the round marks imagined by the early foresters to be none other than the seal of Solomon, the son of David, (on both of whom be peace!) ❧ There is no more exquisite green than the beautiful, shining leaves of this plant, with its tiny white bells of flowers. It has a near relative almost always growing near it, that, with singular paucity of imagination, our botanists have called "False Solomon's Seal."

HOW we reveal our mental habits through this trick we have of falsifying the plants. We say "false" asphodel, "false" rice, "false" hellebore, "false" spikenard and mitrewort, but the falsity is in our own vain imaginings. The plants are as true as the earth that bears them, or the rain and the sunshine that bring them to perfection. The Solomon's seal is one lily, the "false" Solomon's seal another. Man may be false, "perilous Godheads of choosing" are his, but the wild things of the woods are true, each in the order of its nature ❧ There are no complexities or subtilities about wake-robin, here by the streamside. You may see it at a glance, for its principles are brief and fundamental, as wise old Marcus Aurelius bids us let our own be, and yet, the plant has had its vicissitudes; has met and solved its problems. Reasoning from analogies, time must have been when, like others of its great family, it grew in the water, floating out its broad leaves, lolling at ease on the surface of swampy, watery places and still ponds. Times changed. Lands rose and waters subsided, and wake-robin found itself in the midst of new conditions. The problem of self-support confronted it, and the plant solved it by divesting from its broad, sustaining sepals nutriment to enable the long, swaying stem to meet the new demands upon it. It still loves water and seeks cool, damp woods and deep canyons, growing beside little streams where it lifts its face to greet the springtime. It is probably not so big as when it rested luxuriously upon the water, but it is wake-robin, still, and it does more than summon the birds: it calls each of us back to Nature, bidding us keep our hearts and souls alive to see, with each renewing of springtime, and to love afresh, the miracles of Nature's redemptive force.

HE beauty of springtime, like the beauty of childhood, is always new. All about me the things of Nature are still in the mystical, subtile tenderness of their young, green growth. The golden days of autumn are full of their own beauty. The grey days of winter's mist and fog have theirs, but there is something in the tender blue days of the rainy springtime that sets the heart apraise, and brings out as nothing else can, the meanings of leaf and bud, of flower and tree. It is raining, now. Up above me, on the road, several picnickers who have been caught in this April shower are hurrying to shelter. They look down curiously at me, here under the willow, and I have some misgiving as to whether they are not setting an example that I should follow. But I am sure that it is a great mistake always to know enough to go in when it rains. One may keep snug and dry by such knowledge, but one misses a world of loveliness. There is, after all, a certain selective wisdom that sees the desirability of taking the showers as they come.

HERE is something peculiarly tender and loving about an April shower. One is so fully conscious, even while the drops are falling, that the sun is shining behind the light clouds. And the drops themselves come down so gently, tentatively offering themselves, as it were, to the welcoming earth—pattering lightly on the leaves, and softly rippling the surface of the little pool under the willows. That is a wonderful sort of comparison the Hebrew poet gives us when he likens the teaching of truth to the small rain upon the tender herb: the showers upon the green grass

The young colt in the stall, yonder, thrusts an eager head over the half-door, and with soft black muzzle in the air, stands with open mouth to catch the delicious trickle. The cattle on the hills seem glad of the wetting. Even the birds have not sought shelter, and why should I? I love to watch the leaves of the trees and plants, in the rain. They tell us so many secrets about the life of which they are a part. Why, for instance, does this pond lily spread out its broad, pleasant leaves upon the water's surface, while its cousin the brodeia has long, narrow, grass-like leaves? Why do the leaves of the pungent wormwood, here, stand rigidly pointing upwards, while those of this big oak are spread out before the descending rain?

WATCH the wormwood. See how the raindrops quiver for an instant on the tips of the pinnate leaves, then follow one another in a mad chase down the groove that traverses the center of each leaf. Notice that the leaf itself rises from three ridges on the stem of the plant, and that between these ridges lie shallow grooves down which the raindrops run to the plant's root. Now, we can tell from these signs what sort of a root the wormwood has. I never pulled one of the plants, but I am sure that if we were to do so we should find it to have a main tap-root, with no branches. All such plants have leaves pointing upwards, and grooved stems, admirably adapted to bring water to the thirsty roots. The beets and the radishes afford us capital examples of this provision

This alfileria has another arrangement of leaf, for this same purpose. It is a widely spreading forage-plant, with an absurdly small root,

It needs a great deal of moisture, and so its stems are thickly set with soft, fuzzy hairs, that catch the water and convey it to the root ❧ Growing all along the bank is the little chickweed, with its tiny white star of a blossom. If it were not so common we should wax enthusiastic over its beauty, and seek it for our garden borders. It has a running, thread-like root, which receives the raindrops caught by the stem in a single row of tiny hairs along its lower side, and sprinkled gently down.

WHEN a plant has a spreading root such as the willow, yonder, sends down, the leaves spread outward and downward, from base to tip, letting their gathered moisture down upon it. When the plant grows under water its leaves are long and threadlike; for the supply of carbon is limited, and they divide minutely, that the greatest possible surface may be exposed to absorb it. If the stem grows until the leaves reach the surface of the water they broaden and spread out, for here they get an abundant food supply which they may freely appropriate, as none of it need be diverted to build up a supporting stem. The water affords the leaves ample support ❧ The grasses grow in blades for the same reason that the plants growing under water put out slender, thread-like leaves. The air-supply would seem abundant, but the grass-leaves are many, and low-growing plants are numerous. So they divide and sub-divide, that greater surface may be presented to the sunlight and the air. In this form the blades are fittest to obtain their necessary food supply and thus to survive. We see this same tendency in the leaves of the wild poppy, the buttercup and all the great crowfoot family. Across the road stretches a line of locusts, just now in dainty, snowy, fragrant blossom.

The individuality of a tree is a constant and delightful fact in Nature. The locust is as unlike the oak or the willow as can well be imagined, yet like them in taking on an added and characteristic loveliness in the rain. How delicately the branches pencil themselves against the blue and silver of the cloudy sky and the dark green of the orchard beyond them! The leaves have such a purely incidental air. The lines of the tree were, themselves, lovely enough in their green and mossy wetness, to delight the eye. To deck them so laceywise in an openwork of leaf and blossom was beneficent gratuity on the part of Mother Nature, for the pleasing of her children.

DOWN below, where the creek widens, the sycamores have grown to great size. How they help the heart, these gnarly giants, with the white patches against the greys and blacks of their rough trunks! How they spread their branches against the sky and beckon and point the beholder upwards. The sylvan prophet bears a promise of good, and demands of every passer-by the query of the wise old stoic: "Who is he that shall hinder thee from being good and simple?"

Over the rounded hill, stealing softly, in Indian file, through the mist, a row of eucalyptus trees climb, fringing up the slopes. These ladies of the hilltop have a fashion of growing thus, and in no other position is their delicate, suggestive beauty more apparent. The eucalyptus is an original genius among trees, never repeating itself. It stands for endless variety, for strong good cheer, for faith that seeks and reaches and goes on, never wavering ❧ It blesses as well as delights its friends. I love its wonderful, ever varying leaves, its upreaching, outstretching branches, and the annual surprise of its mystic blossoming. Each tree is distinct and individual in its growth, yet every one is typical of the genus.

IT IS a tree of the wind and the storm. See how those in yonder group sway and courtesy, bow and beckon, advance and retreat in the light breeze! And the rain does such marvels to them in the way of color, tinting the leaves into wondrous things of glistening black-and-silver, and bringing out exquisite, evasive greens and browns, red and rose colors, tender blues and greys, from the trunks and branches ☘
All the things of Nature are for man's use and joy, but perhaps they serve their very highest use when we return God thanks for their beauty ❧
Yes, I am sure that there is a wisdom wiser than the prudence which sends us in out of the rain. The flowers and the grasses teach

us more than has ever been put between the covers of books. The trees bring us the real news of the real world long before they are crushed into pulp and made into the paper on which is printed our morning service from the scandal monger and the stock broker. It was heralded as a marvelous triumph of modern ingenuity when, the other day, a forest tree was cut down and made into paper on which the news of the world was printed and hawked along the streets within four and one-half hours from the moment when the axe was laid at the root of the tree. Marvelously clever, that, but shall we ever be wise enough to bring the trees themselves to the city, instead? If we were but able to read the message they bear, the newspaper might go away into outer darkness, whence it sprang.

THERE is a fearful moment of reckoning before us should it ever chance that when all our trees shall have been sacrificed on the altar of the patron-fiend of news, the newspaper supply shall suddenly be cut off and we find ourselves some fine morning minus our tidbits of shame and failure and disaster, left to the companionship of our own thoughts ☘ Dante never imagined a terror like this ❧

But the sun has come out again. The rain is

over and gone. Only the last treasured drops chase one another along the leaves and down the stems of the plants. Our picnickers are venturing forth ❧ The wet blades of grass sparkle in the sunlight. Over on the bank a ruby-throated hummer is flying back and forth across a tiny stream that patters and splashes against a rock. These morsels of birds love a shower-bath and this fellow now has one exactly to his mind. The clouds have drifted down the sky and everything seems glad and grateful for "the useful trouble of the rain."

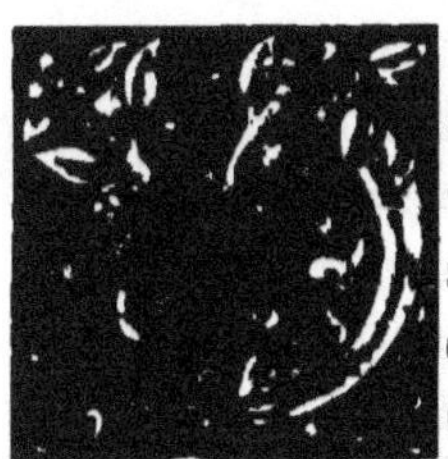

NCE upon a time man conceived the belief that this universe, with its many worlds swinging through space, was created for him. He fancied that the sun shone by day to warm and vivify him; that the stars of night were none other than lamps to his feet; that the other animals existed to afford him food and clothing—and sport; that the very flowers of the field blossomed and fruited and were beautiful for his gratification. In fact, man conceived the belief that instead of being the wise brother and helper of this creation amidst which he moves, he was the great central pivot upon which all revolves ☘

A sorry lesson, surely, for man to read into the broad, open page of Nature's great book. Small wonder that to him in his meanness its message came as "the painful riddle of the earth." But it was the best he could do: it is the best any of us can do until we have learned the great lesson which the ancient Wise One has written out for us—which she will teach us, in time, through death, if we will not let her teach it through life: the lesson that use is not appropriation; that appropriation sets use to groan and sweat under fardels of evil ❧

We are learning this lesson, with a bad grace,

like blundering school boys, fumbling at our hornbook, stuttering and stammering over the alphabet of life, the while our minds wander stupidly off to the playthings of our unholy civilization. Perhaps some day we shall spell out something of this riddle which we have made so painful, and with the lesson get somewhat of the humility that comes with knowing

But now man does not read the book of Nature to much better purpose than he reads those other volumes, written by himself, and bought by himself, in bulk, to adorn his libraries: portly tomes to which he may point with pride as evidence that at least his shelves hold wisdom, tho' his head may never.

I USE no figure of speech when I say that we may now buy our books in bulk. I saw, only this morning, the advertisement of a large dry goods "emporium" ('tis laces and literature now) wherein is announced for sale the bound volumes of a popular magazine. "Over eight pounds of the choicest reading, bound in the usual style—olive green."

Nature has olive greens, too, in styles usual and unusual, and she has marvelous messages for her lovers, but she cannot be bought in bulk, nor put upon shelves, nor even carried in the head until she first be received into the heart A little flaxen haired girl brought me, this morning, a pure white buttercup on the stem with three yellow ones.

"See," she said, "Here is one buttercup they forgot to paint."

I took the flower from her hand. I could not tell her just how it happened that this one perianth was white, but I explained to her something of how the others came to be yellow What we call a flower is not, usually, the flower at all, but merely its petals. The real flower is the cluster, in the center of the calyx, of pistils and their surrounding pollen-bearing stamens. Away back in the ages when man had not yet developed his æsthetic sense, perhaps even before he had learned to make fire, the primitive flower bore only these pistils and stamens, with a little outer protective whorl of green petals. It was fertilized by the pollen falling upon the pistils.

BUT this was not good for the plant. Those flowers that in some way became fertilized by pollen from other plants of the same variety, by cross-fertilization, in fact, were healthier and stronger than those fertilized by their own pollen. In such plants as wind-blown pollen reached this cross-fertilization was an easy matter, but the buttercup is not one of these. It is forced to rely upon insects for fertilization.

So the plant began to secrete a sweet drop at the base of each green petal. Such insects as discovered this nectar and stopped to sip were dusted with the pollen of the plant and carried it to other flowers, where it fertilized the pistils, the insect gathering from every blossom a fresh burden of pollen to be carried along on his nectar-seeking round. This was very good, so far as it went, but the flowers were pale and inconspicuous, and many of them, overlooked by the insects, were never visited. Certain ones, however, owing to accidents or conditions of soil and moisture, had the calyx a little larger, or brighter colored than their fellows, and these the insects found. It happened, therefore, if anything ever does merely happen, that the flowers with bright petals were fertilized, and their descendants were even brighter colored. Thus, in time, the buttercup, by the process which, for lack of a better name, we call natural selection, came to have bright yellow petals, because these attract the insect best adapted to fertilize it ❧ If man's æsthetic sense is gratified by the flower's beauty, why man is by so much the better off, but that man is pleased by the bright color is not half so important to the buttercup as is the pleasure of a certain little winged beetle which sees the shining golden cup and knows that it means honey ☘ In the same way the lupin, yonder, with its pretty blue and white blossoms, has developed its blue petals because it is fertilized by the bees. They seek it as they do other blossoms, not only for honey, but for the pollen itself, which stands them in place of bread ☙ The very shape of the flower is due to the visits of countless generations of this insect. The bee is the insect best adapted to fertilize the lupin, and when he alights upon the threshold of a blossom his weight draws the lower petal down, and entering to suck the sweets he gets his head dusted with pollen. If a fly were to gain entrance to the flower, he would carry away no pollen. He is smaller than the bee, and his head could not reach it. So honey-seeking flies alight in vain; their weight is not enough to press the calyx open, so they may not enter and drink of its sweets. Yonder on a blossom of the mimulus, the odd-looking monkey-plant, a honeybee just had this same experience. The bumblebee is the only insect that is large enough to reach the pollen in this blossom, and so its doors will open only to him. Botanists tell us that all this great family, to which belong the various peas blossoms and their cousins, were once five-petaled plants, but natural selection has brought about their present shape, which is an admirable

protection against the depredations of small insects that could only rob but could not fertilize the flowers

Blue is the favorite color of the honeybee, and next to blue he prefers red. So bee blossoms are blue or red.

MOST of our small white flowers are fertilized by insects that fly at night. This is the reason why white blossoms are more fragrant than their bright-hued sisters. Bright colors could not be seen at night, but the fragrance of the white flowers, always more noticeable by night than by day, serves the same end—to attract the useful insects. This is an essential part of Nature's wonderful plan. The flower lives by giving

There is an endless fascination in this page which Nature opens out before us, in her upland pastures. A wise teacher once told me his experience with a restless, unmanageable boy "I could do nothing with him," the teacher said, "until I got him interested in field life." One day this boy went off on a holiday tramp, returning the day following. His teacher asked him what he had seen, and this is what he remembered of his outing: "I camped in a field for the night," said he, "and I saw a bee light on a poppy and crawl in. The poppy shut up and caught him. Next morning I woke up early and watched, and by and by the poppy opened and the bee came out." ❦ There are those who might have missed the sacred significance of such a narrative, but that teacher was a very wise man and he knew that the reading lesson given him then was a page from his rough boy's soul-life, and he conned it with reverent delight. Life together was more real for them both after that day.

THE keener our realization of the human love that is in the flowers, in the trees, in all the wild life about us, the richer is our humanity, the fuller our reception of life and love, the more thoughtful our use of all the things of Nature becomes ❦ Once I saw an oriole weaving some bits of string into his nest. He hung head downwards, by one string, from a projecting branch, and worked, for nearly an hour, with beak and claws. Then he flew away, triumphant. Later I saw his nest and understood his action. He tied two pieces of string together in a very respectable sort of knot: had wound the long cord thus obtained in and out among the meshes of his nest and then, giving it a half-hitch about a twig, had brought the free end up and tied it securely to another small branch ❦

I felt grateful for what that bird had accomplished. All human achievements seemed to me worthier after seeing him do this thing. Nature teaches us so much if we will but keep still long enough to let her: if we will only empty ourselves of conceit and knowingness, and get rid of the notion that all things, Nature included, are made for us. We are not the lords of creation. We are only a small part, albeit the highest part, of it all, and the better we learn this lesson the better men and women we shall become.

I WAS SITTING here beside the stream, watching the bees swarm in and out at the entrance to their hive, when Hercules passed by. "Come and watch the bees," I called as he passed. "They are interesting." ☙

He stood and studied the busy workers, intent upon the business of their miniature society ☙

"I wonder," he said at last, "if our human reason shall ever evolve a system half so perfect as the one that mere instinct has taught these feeble insects." As I was silent he continued:

"Well, at all events, I can learn one lesson from the bees, and be about my business. If society is ever to be freed from its burdens every soul must do its full duty. One life wasted means a whole world hindered just that much." And Hercules was gone to his labors ☙

How fearful we all are of wasting our lives, yet so rarely fearful for the results of the ceaseless activity with which we crowd them ☙ But Hercules' words are full of suggestiveness. Is our boasted human reason really less adequate to the needs of our life than is what we call the instinct, this thing that looks so much more reasonable than our reason, of the lower orders? What if, after all, we are making a desperate mistake in supposing that it is this faculty which we call reason that distinguishes us from the brute creation?

IT IS because the bees and the other dumb creatures have nothing more than this measure of reason which we call instinct, that it serves them perfectly. Man has something else, that draws him higher; that prompts him further. But alas for us! With the destiny to live perfectly as human beings, we yet long for the restrictions through which we may live perfectly as the beasts. We seek our lessons from the brutes while the Eternal waits to teach us. We cannot live like the beasts. The divine human spark within us will not let us. We must live higher than they or we shall live lower, for our perfection of order is infinitely higher than theirs, and our failure immeasurably lower than they can sink

But we go on, we modern Athenians, seeking to ameliorate the conditions we have brought upon society by our own stupid disobedience and inhumanity, and only now and then do we have a faint suspicion that our newest thoughts are but mere rephrasings of ideas old as thought itself.

Men get these new sets of phrases and dress therein the ideas that underlie the universe. We apply the terms of science to the old faiths and think we have invented a new religion. We find new names for God Himself, and believe ourselves to have discovered a new life-principle. Loving the neighbor becomes enlightened altruism, and lo, faith is born anew, with a subtiler power to redeem the world.

HERCULES is a Socialist. He always spells society with a great S, and he declares that in the present state of Society we can take no thought for individuals. "The individual may perish," he says, in moments of eloquence, "but the integrity of Society must be jealously maintained."

I wonder, as I sit here watching the bees, whether Society might not, after all, find easement from its ails if each individual of us, myself and Hercules included, should pay strict attention to our individual business of growing, or becoming humanized?

Just here at my hand a bee has alighted and is burying its nose in a clover blossom. Here is an example of a life that is lived only for Society, yet so important is the individual in the opinion of this highly perfected body social, that I have seen half a dozen bees, when a laden worker has arrived at the hive opening, weighted down, too exhausted to do other than drop, helpless, upon the threshold, rush to its assistance, relieve it of its heavy load and help it to pass within to gather strength for further effort. The strict individualist complains, in turn, of the bees because they have no individual life; no existence separate from the hive. This is true, but what higher individuality can any creature desire than is comprised and summed up in the divine opportunity to bring his individual gift to the common store?

I HAVE picked the clover blossom that the bee just left. Beside it are growing other blossoms, and I gather a couple. They are the veriest wayside weeds—dandelion and dog-fennel—but they are important because they are typical representatives of the largest order in the floral kingdom; an order which, although it was the last to appear in the vegetable world, has outstripped every other and leads them all today. Botanists call it the Composite Order. Its members are really floral socialists, just as Hercules and the rest of us who believe that government is an order of nature, and good for the race, are human socialists, whether we know it or not.

BUT most of us hold a mistaken idea about the relation of the individual to the whole. We are apt to theorize that it is the duty of the individual to keep the whole in order, and a good many of us are fully convinced that the world owes us a living. So it does, and it behooves each one of us to be faithful in discharging his individual share of the aggregate debt. Nature has a whole page about that in her wonderful volume.

Take, for instance, this clover. What we call the blossom is, in reality, many blossoms. Look at the mass under a glass. You will see that the clover head is made up of numerous minute cups in a compact cluster. Each cup is a perfect blossom. As we now see it in the clover it is a tiny tube, but it once possessed five slender petals which are now united. The little pointed scollops that rim the cup suggest these petals. Now, the tiny cup is descended from a five-petaled ancestor, growing upon its individual stem and depending upon insects for its fertilization. The flower was small, however, and many of them must have been overlooked by the insects.

But those blossoms that, growing very close

together, formed little clusters, were more conspicuous than the solitary ones, and were discovered, visited for their honey and incidentally fertilized by the winged freebooters. These blossoms bore fruit and their descendants inherited the social instinct prompting them to draw together that each might give the other its help and co-operation in attracting the insects. So, by degrees, the co-operative habit became fixed in the clover, and in many other plants, until the compositæ became a botanical fact. In other words, the individuals formed a body social of their own, growing from a compact cluster from a common stem, each giving and receiving, constantly, its use and share in the common life. The many-petaled flowers found it inconvenient to arrange themselves in the composite order, and so, as we see in the clover, the petals have pressed closely together and united to form a tube-shaped flower, and as the tubular form is best adapted to receive fertilization by the bee, which insect is the most useful to the clover blossom, that form has been perpetuated in this plant.

THUS by the simple process of each individual giving itself to the common life, the mutual protection and development of the whole, this order of plants has become the largest in the floral kingdom. The compositæ have circled the globe. They fill our hothouses and flourish in our gardens; they greet us by the dusty road, and in the summer woods. The lovely golden-rod, the sturdy asters, the aristocratic chrysanthemums, the dainty daisies all belong to this great order. So does helianthus, the big, beaming sunflower.

IT is quite true that each blossom of the compositæ has given its life to the race. But what if, after all, life with our fellows is a giving instead of the receiving we are wont to think it?

What if, after all, the true outlook upon Society will one day show us that our neighbor is put here that we may have the great, the inestimable joy of living for him?

All matter is made up of molecules, Science tells us, and there is another Voice as of one having authority, which tells us that One hath made of one blood all nations of men for to dwell upon the face of the earth

We humans are but larger molecules in the body social. We live only in so far as the common life flows through us. We never fully, in our plans, and by a wonderful provision of Divine Wisdom we cannot give one another that which is really and unmistakably our own. No human thought, even, ever traveled a straight course from one human

soul to another and was received exactly as it was sent. We live our lives each within the molecular envelope of his individual body, and we can no more mix, in reality, than the molecules mix. We live only in the flux and reflux of the Life of all, and only as we pass this on have power to receive.

IT is when life is fullest that we turn to our fellows. Those of us who are true know that then we need them most, and so, our real drawings together are in order that we may give. We know this in that secret part of us where lies what most of us call our human weakness, but we are faithless to the knowledge, and choose to live on a lower plane, within that outer circle which we call knowing. We think we come together to receive, but who of us does not know the emptiness of death that lies in such coming? We are all a little better than this. In secret we know that it is more blessed to give than receive, but we are ashamed of the knowledge.

We are less simple and true than the dandelion, the dog-fennel and the sweet-clover here in the grass. The small common blossoms grow so cheerily one is glad to come back to them. It is true that not one wee tube or strap or head in any cluster could have much life outside the aggregate blossom, but the integrity and perfection of each is an essential factor in the integrity and perfection of the whole. The tiny single flower that I can pull from this dandelion seems but an insignificant speck, but, by and by, could it have been let alone, it would, its ripeness and perfection attained, have taken to itself wings and sailed fluffily off upon the breeze to renew its life perhaps a thousand miles from here. Seeing it float through the air a poet might have found it a theme for a sonnet. A scientist might have seen universal law embodied in its structure, or a seer have reasoned from it to life eternal.

YET, but for the co-operation of its fellows in the body floral, it could not have lived any more than, save for its fellows, what we know as the dandelion could have lived. The law of co-operation, like all of Nature's laws, makes for rightness and fitness all along the line. She teaches us, with ever-repeated emphasis, the lesson of independence of kind. The isolated being is, everywhere, the comparatively helpless being. The tree growing by itself in the open field often attains to more symetrical perfection and beauty than the tree in the crowded forest, but woodmen tell us that the forest tree makes better timber. We must live with and for our fellows, but he does this best who, in the quiet order of the common life, opens widest his soul to the Source thereof, and growing to the full stature of a man helps on to perfection what should be that composite flower of the race, our human civilization.

HE little spring here gushes up and then sweeps away along a stony bed overgrown with brakes and tares. On its margin, amid a tangle of wild blackberry, I have come upon a forest of scouring-rush ❦
It is a quaint growth. I love to put my face close to the earth and, looking through the rushes' green stems, to fancy myself a wee brownie, wandering among a ☘ dense wilderness of pines. The development of the miniature trees is an interesting process ❦ First the ground is covered with slender brown fingers ❦ thrusting up through the soil. These grow rapidly, and in a few days spread out their brief, verticillate branches to the breeze, as proudly as any great tree might do. Here is a tiny finger just pointing upward; yonder towers the giant of the liliputian forest, ful-

ly half-a-foot high. "Scouring-weed," says the farmer, contemptuously, "they aint no good. Some call 'em horsetail."

IN fact, the queer, witchy little things have a number of names: candle-rush, scouring-rush, horsetail, and their own proper appellation, equisitum. I have gathered a number of the little trees and they lie side by side in my palm while my mind tries to recall a few of the facts that go to make up the plant's wonderful history. Our grandmothers used to strew their floors with it, that no careless tread might soil the snowy boards. They used it, as well, for scouring, hence its name. Those who seek correspondences between the natural and physical kingdoms find the rush an emblem of cleansing, and this is precisely the office which, since earliest creation, it has filled for the world. For our scouring-rush was not always the puny, insignificant thing we see it. It belongs to the carboniferous age. It has nothing to do with our modern civilization. It had reached its highest perfection and entered upon its downward career before man appeared on the earth. Its progenitors flourished with the giant ferns, the great, rank mosses, and all the rest of the carbon-storing vegetation. A mighty tree was our little rush in those days, growing several hundred feet tall and spreading out its huge whorls of branches in every direction. So we find it today, in the anthracite beds of the eastern slope. What happened to it that we should know it, living, as this degenerate creature of the bog?

IN the carboniferous age the air surrounding the earth was much warmer than at present, warmer than we find it in the tropics. The great mass which constitutes this globe was not yet cool enough to support any very high forms of life. There were no trees, as we now understand the word, and there was very little animal life. Beetles crawled about, spiders and scorpions, and salamanders big as alligators, but there were no mammals, no birds ❧ The world was in twilight, reeking with moisture, steaming in the warm air which it filled with all sorts of noxious gases. It rained aquafortis and brimstone, and the sweating earth sent these up again in deadly fog-banks of poisonous vapor ❧

These were the conditions that our big rush loved. Its huge spongy stem and branches drank in life from the death-laden atmosphere. Its great creeping rootstocks soaked it up from the morass beneath and the rush grew luxuriantly. Its office was indeed a cleansing one, to purify the atmosphere and make it fit to sustain animal life. In time, as the huge primeval trees reached maturity, they died, and the mighty stems fell back in the bog. Then came some great upheaval, some cataclysm of nature such as we find everywhere recorded in her rocky books. The land rose or sank, and the rocks and debris of the sea floor were thrown upon the decaying vegetation. It was pressed and compressed beneath this weight. The fronds of the huge ferns; the tall stems of the giant rushes; the monstrous club-mosses, and the primeval forest became a peat-bog. Still greater pressure—a longer lapse of aeons, and the peat became coal.

WE burn them now, in our grates, the progenitors of these feeble things lying here, limply, in my palm. Is it not, as I said, a wonderful history the frail thing has. A degenerate stock, botanists call it. So are its cousins the ferns degenerate, with no botanical Nordau to sound warning against them. But degenerates tho' they all are, they have still the spirit of the pioneer. They dwell in the outposts of vegetable civilization. We do not find them flourishing where Nature is in her gentlest moods ❧ Once, down in the crater of an active volcano, half-a-mile from any soil, growing from a sulphur-stained black-lava floor, I found a clump of waving green ferns, as high as my head, spreading out their broad fronds as though to cover and hide the terrible nakedness of the unfinished earth. A thousand years from now a grain-field may spread where now those frail green plumes have just begun their gracious work.

HIS clothing of the earth and the cleansing of the air are the tasks the giant rushes helped to perform for the young world. During the process the rank gases of the atmosphere were gradually stored up within their great stems. Liberated, now, in our grates and retorts they give us heat and light. Then, the atmosphere becoming purer, the earth cooled and life sustaining, new growths appeared. All the conditions were improved, but the improvement meant death to the big rush. It was starving. It could not find food in the thin air. Its roots could not suck up enough moisture to sustain life. It became smaller and smaller. Flowers and seeds it had never borne. It now gave up its leaves. Between every two whorls of branches on the scouring-rush we find a little brown, toothed sheath encircling the stem. In the days of the plants' prosperity each of these teeth was a leaf, but now the rush can maintain no such extravagance as leaves, so there remain only these poor survivals. The stem is hollow, and is divided, between the whorls of branches, into closed sections, or

joints. It has also an outer ring of hollow tubes, through which moisture is drawn up from the soil, to feed the branches. The rush is a little higher order of creation than the fern, but it is a cryptogram; that is, a plant never bearing true seeds, but propagating by spores

And so, fallen upon hard lines, chilled, stunted by the cold, but having a brief span of life when the spring rains have made the earth wet and warm, and before the summer heat has come to wither it, we have our scouring-rush only a few inches high.

AND this branched stem which we see is not fertile. 'Tis enough for it to support its waving green feather. The fertile stems are not branched. They appear above the earth, pale and shrinking; put forth no branches, but live a brief season, develop their spores and disappear

The growth of the scouring-rush seems to me to show something beautiful, as well as interesting. There is a certain light-hearted gaiety in the waving, tree-like thing which makes one forget that it is a degenerate stock, and doomed to destruction. Still a little work remains for it to do: still some waste places and miasmatic bogs to be cleansed and purified, and so the little rush grows on, the merest shadow of its once opulent self. I am sure that the last horsetail to be seen on earth will grow just as breezily, as greenly and as cheerily as any now waving in this make-believe enchanted forest at my feet.

And who knows what may be the fate of that which was the real life of that ancient plant, —the forces of light and heat set free in our furnaces and forges, to begin, again, their office of ministering use?

Did the giant rush die? Does anything die? Ages have seen the rushes fall and pass from sight, to wake to glorious light in the leaping flames. We see leaves fall each year and turn to mold from which other life-forms spring. There will be other poppies, next year, where yonder orange-red blossoms nod in the breeze. The waving grain, already headed out and bowing under its burden of raindrops, was but a few months since a mere handful of dry kernels. They were cast upon the ground, and they died, if that tossing sea of green is death. We see these things recurring upon every side of us, yet we still go up and down the earth demanding of prophet, priest and poet: "If a man die shall he live again?"

A far cry from the little sprigs of scouring-rush in my hand? But Life is a far cry, from Everlasting through Eternity, and who shall say, of the least of these, its manifestations, "It is no good?"

OWN among the water-cresses, an hour ago, studying the movements of a mammoth slug, I was startled by a shadow that fell directly across my hands. At the same moment there was an excited flurry and scurrying to shelter, among a tuneful mob of songsparrows who, all unmindful of my presence, were teetering close beside me upon the tall mustard stalks that swayed beneath their weight

Looking upward I saw, between me and the sun, a pigeon-hawk soaring on motionless wings in the freedom of the upper air. I watched him with a joy that had no touch of envy, as he circled widely against the sky, rising, falling, swerving, returning, with scarcely a dip of the strong, outstretched wings

High though he poised, my thought could reach him; strong though his flight, my fancy could follow and outstrip him. He, high above the mountain-tops, gazed downward to the earth. His thoughts, his desires were here. To materialize them he mounted the air. With my feet upon the earth; with no palpable pinions wherewith to climb the ether, yet have I moments of being, more trusty than he, a creature of the sky

OMETHING of this ☘ passed through my brain as I watched the circling hawk. Once, with a flash of his strong wings, he made a downward turn and, swift and still, he dropped earthward ❧ Then, as if frustrated in whatever had been his design, he wheeled again and climbed as swiftly up the air ❧

I like that phrase as describing the flight of a bird. It is so literally what the creature does. A bird is not superior to gravitation. But for that force he would be the helpless victim of every little breeze, like a balloon, which is unable to shape a course or do anything but float helplessly before the wind. The balloon floats because it is lighter than the air, but the air which the bird displaces is lighter than he, and he only moves in it by virtue of his ability to extract from it, by the motion of his wings, sufficient recoil to propel himself forward. He rises, as do we humans, by means of that which resists him ❧

I love to watch the seagulls. They do this so perfectly, and seem to delight to give us lessons in ærial navigation as they dip and whirl and call about the steamers, on the Bay. Their wings are so easy to study while in action. The first joint, to where the wing bends back and outward, is strong and compact, cup shaped underneath. The second joint tapers. The feathers are long and do not overlap so closely as do those of the first joint, and at the free end they spread out and turn upward. The upper surface of the wing is convex, the lower surface concave. In flying the wings are thrown forward and downward. Flying is not a flapping of the wings up and down, and if a bird were to strike its wings backward and downward, as its manner of flight is so often pictured, it would turn a forward somersault in the air.

STRUCTURALLY the wing of a bird is a screw. It twists in opposite directions during the up and down strokes, and describes a figure of 8 in the air. The bird throws its wings forward and downward. The air is forced back and compressed in the cup-shaped hollows of the wings, and these latter, by the recoil thus obtained, drag the body forward. This resistance of the air is absolutely essential to flight. We who think that, but for the buffetings of hard fate, we, too, might soar high and fly free in the upper realm of endeavor, should watch the efforts of the birds in a calm. We shall scarcely see them flying. If impelled to flight, by necessity, the process is a most laborious one. There being no resisting wind on which to climb (birds always fly against the wind) the climber must, by the rapid action of his wings, establish a recoil that will send him along. Watch the little mud-hen, flying close to the surface of the water, ready to dive the instant its timidity takes fright. Its wings vibrate swiftly, unceasingly, for it rarely rises high enough above the water to have advantage of the air currents. For it there are no long, soaring sweeps through the air; no freedom from the labors of its cautious flight. It is a very spendthrift of effort because of the timidity that never lets it rise to the sustaining forces just above its head. To climb the sky is not for him who hugs cover.

TO FLY! The very thought sets the nerves atingle. It is joy to be afloat, "with a wet sheet and a flowing sea and a wind that follows fast." It is a joy to be on the back of a swiftly running horse, with the wind rushing away from your face as you ride, bearing every care from your brain ❧ But to traverse the air—to fly! This joy we long for: we have an indisputable, an inalienable right to long for it. To what heights may we rise? This, after all, is the question that concerns us. Sordid, creeping wights that we are, constantly referring our heavenward aspiration to the desire of the mortal, we still

"To man propose this test—
Thy body, at its best,
How far can that project its soul on its lone way?"

OUR VERY protests, our kicking against the pricks that would incite us to higher effort are but our blind fear lest, after all, they should not mean flight. We are afraid of our moments of faith; ashamed of our aspiring impulse, the upward impulse that throbbed through all life since the world was born. We send forward our souls if haply they should find God, while we remain behind to weigh and test their evidence when they return to us—if they ever do, hugging the surface the while, lest a sustaining breath of spiritual force lift us clean above the safe shelter in which we may dive altogether should our returning souls bring back news of the meanings of life, scaring us to cover, after all, by the thought that we ourselves, are heaven and hell

Usually we are content to grovel. We traverse our little round and declare it to be destiny. We prate of the limitations of our humanity, forgetful of that humanity's limitless capacity to receive. With insincere self-abasement we declare ourselves to be worms of the dust, and the spirits of light who look upon us may readily believe our assertions ❧

But there are moments when the scales fall from our eyes. We get fleeting glimpses, then, of the meaning and the end of our human nature. We know that it is in the skies. We know that we have ourselves fashioned the chain that binds us to earth. We know that we were made for flight, and we know that we know all this. Still afar in the sky the hawk soars, with downward gaze seeking his desire. Still, tho' my feet are upon the earth, my spirit fares upward in its flight toward its desire, above and beyond its strong wings' farther-est flight.

WONDER whether the restless impulse that sends city folks hillward in the springtime is not a part of the Divine Plan that would lead us all to lift up our eyes to the hills whence our help cometh. They flock up here, the city folks, during these first spring days, to eat their luncheons by the roadside and to fill their hands with the poppies and wild hyacinth, the blue-eyed grass and pimpernel that everywhere dot the young meadows' glowing green. I hear, at night-fall, mother's voices calling the little ones to prepare for home-going, and I love to see the contented parties go wandering down, the tiniest tired climber usually sound asleep in his father's arms with the sun's last rays caressing the small face. It is good for them to be here. There is, in the dumbest of us, a faint stirring of recognition that the hope and promise of life are in the young year. This love of the childhood of things is the best thing our human nature knows: the best because there is in it the least of self. It is a different thing from the love of new beginnings. It is not new beginnings, but first principles that the soul seeks, now, and so we climb the hills, as naturally as the daisies look upward, leaving behind us the pitiful aims that end in self and belong to the dead level.

IN THE springtime love awakens, born anew in the green wonder of the season's childhood. Yonder where the road climbs the hill the sunlight is sifting in long bars through the eucalyptus trees, making a brown and golden ladder all along the way. In everything is the fresh, tender suggestion of a Sunday afternoon in the springtime. The air is full of the scent of swamp-willow and laurel, and the breath of feeding cattle on the hills

By the roadside He and She walk shyly apart. They could scarcely clasp hands across the space that separates them, yet one seeing them knows their hearts are close together. The blue sky arches over them: the soft clouds pass lightly above their heads: the sunbeams bring brighter rounds for the brown and golden ladder his feet and hers tread lightly. They are palpably "of the people." Her hands are roughened and red from toil. His shoulders are bent by the early bearings of heavy burdens. Neither He nor She is over twenty years old, and they are poor, as some count riches, but to them, together, has come the sweetness of life, and He and She are walking on the heights

ESTERDAY they were but a boy and a girl, but today He to her is Manhood; She, to him, is Womanhood, and in this great human wilderness they have reached out and found each other. Could anything be more wonderful than this? Could anything exceed in beauty this secret of theirs that he who runs may read in every line of their illumined faces?

Students versed in the 'ologies: sociologists, philanthropists, economists and progressionists of every sort, we know all that you would say. We have heard your arguments time and again. We have listened to your statistics and watched the shaking of your head over these unions of the poor. But the wisdom of life is wiser than men, else He and She would do well to listen to you instead of walking together here on the hill road. They do not know these things that we are seeking to reduce to what we call social science; and if they should know them, what then? Are they not of more value than many sparrows?

The afternoon shadows lengthen. Home-going groups are beginning the long descent. The voices of little children calling to one another

ing silverly over the hillside. He and She are not hastening. They have loitered along to where a bend in the road affords a wide outlook upon the city below, the gleaming bay, the white-winged ships coming in through the Golden Gate, the distant hills. In her hand are some poppies which he gathered.

DOWN to the western horizon sinks the sun. The gold has faded from the road, leaving it a winding ribbon of grey. The crests of the hills and the gently swelling uplands are flooded with crimson light. It touches the eucalyptus trees into glory and flames in splendor along the western sky. It lights her face and his as they stand transformed before each other. They do not know that the crimson light has made them beautiful. They think the beauty each sees is the other's, a part of their wonderful discovery, and who shall say that either is wrong? It is we who are blind, and not love. Indeed, love, alone, sees clearly. External, temporal conditions have made his body less than noble; have crossed his face with dull, heavy lines. They have narrowed her mental horizon and imprisoned her soul in a poor little cage, but He and She are held above these, now. They have been touched by the finger of God, and have seen each other's beauty, the beauty that is their human right; that once seen is never, again, wholly lost.

HE crimson has faded to rose, the rose to wonderful green—the green has turned to white. The early moon has come out to light the hill. Hand in hand they are passing down the road. Hand in hand they are going through life, toiling together, bearing together the burdens Fate brings to them. They know not what these may be. It is not given them to know the future, or by taking thought to lighten its ills or explain the blunders that have heaped these up. They have no strength or power, but to them has been given love

Will love be theirs when Spring is gone and the summer drouth is upon them; when Autum's harvest time is passed them by and Winter's breath has chilled their blood? Will love be theirs when, hand in hand, in the uncertain white light, they journey down the hill of life?

The cynic smiles at the question. The scientist deprecates it. Philanthropist and sociologist shake their heads

Let it pass. Love is their's now. The universe

is theirs, for each to each is universal. The Life of the universe is in them, and in the shimmering radiance that lights the way, silvering the city and making long, shining paths across the distant water as they go walking down the hill road.

SO HERE THEN ENDETH UPLAND ☘
PASTURES BY ADELINE KNAPP AS
PRINTED BY ME, ELBERT HUBBARD,
AT THE ROYCROFT PRINTING SHOP
IN EAST AURORA, NEW YORK, U. S. A.